The Fragrance of Love

The Fragrance of Love

Susan Mellon

Editing: Precision Editing Group
Cover: Brenda Walter
Formatting: Blue Valley Author Services
ISBN: 9781088721377
1-0887-2137-0

To my Aunt Sally, for always being there

Also available by Susan Mellon
The Locket

TABLE OF CONTENTS

CHAPTER ONE

"**A**ND THE WEATHER TODAY WILL be sunny, with a thirty-percent chance of rain later in the day," the weatherman announced over the radio.

"Bor – ing," Zinnia sang out. She reached down to turn the station. Keeping one eye on the road and the other on the dial, she continued turning it, skipping over channels. Suddenly she heard the familiar voice of Annie Lennox sing out, "*Sweet dreams are made of this*" and she removed her hand from the dial, cranking up the volume. "Sing it, Annie!" Zinnia yelled and slowed her car to a stop at the red light. She sang along while she waited.

Reaching down, Zinnia grabbed her coffee, wanting to take a sip. Just as the liquid touched her lips, her car was hit from behind. The car jolted forward, making her spill the light brown liquid on the front of her white blouse.

"What *in* the world!" she yelled, putting her car into park and setting her cup back into the cupholder. She

1

looked down at her brand-new blouse. "Unbelievable," she mumbled.

While walking around her red Volkswagen Beetle she assessed the damage, letting her fingers glide over the back bumper. She looked at the car that hit hers, noticing a dent on the front bumper of the white Cobalt. The man got out of his car and walked toward her.

"You know," she commented sarcastically, "there's this thing called the brake pedal. I don't know … maybe you heard of it?" She crossed her arms, waiting for his reply.

None came.

He had blond wavy hair that was a bit too long for her liking and wore a faded light-blue T-shirt with the word "Pepsi" printed across the chest. Blue jeans and flip flops finished his attire.

"My car seems fine, but I'm afraid yours was damaged," Zinnia added.

"My car," he answered. He looked at the dent and back at Zinnia, shrugging his shoulders. "No worries. That's an old injury." He slipped his hands into the back pockets of his jeans. "And by the way, I'm fully aware of the brake pedal. It's the one on the right … right?" He smiled, rocking on his feet from toes to heels.

"Cute." She smirked.

"No harm done to either car, so no need bothering exchanging info. I'll just take off."

The stranger turned to get back in his car but stopped and looked at her again. "By the way, it was the sun in my eyes. My bad."

"No harm except my new white blouse is covered in coffee. And I'm interviewing people today looking like this." She motioned to her stained blouse.

The traffic light above them turned green, and a parade of cars behind them blew their horns impatiently, while the cars in the opposing lane whizzed past them.

"Yeah, but you wear the coffee *so* well," he sputtered before getting back into his car.

Zinnia stood for a second watching him. With exasperation she threw her arms in the air and got back in her car. "My bad, but you wear the coffee so well," she mimicked.

She drove the rest of the way to her floral shop in silence. Of all the people living in Lower Braxton, a wannabe comedian was the one who had to hit her.

"Men!" She grumbled.

Zinnia loved living in this small northern-Pennsylvania town. She had stumbled across it strictly by accident about two years ago during a girl's-only road trip. She smiled at the memory. Just herself, her best friend Sophie, the open road and several bottles of wine. The city seemed like it was straight out of a Hallmark movie. A quaint small town delivered in a package, neatly wrapped together with a big bow, just waiting for someone to claim it as their own.

That is exactly what Zinnia did.

The small idyllic town had one main street running through the center, and here all the main businesses could be found. Lower Braxton prided itself on its friendliness. It was the sort of town where everyone looked out for each other. There were no big box stores or huge hotel chains. The residents shopped and supported the local stores and liked it that way. If anyone needed a place to stay, there was a sweet B&B close to town that always seemed to have room for one more guest. Whoever was staying there was greeted each morning with homemade baked goods for breakfast.

Lower Braxton was the perfect place to start over and the perfect place for Zinnia to open her floral shop. After her grandmother passed away, leaving her with a sizable inheritance, she knew what she was going to do. The two of them talked endlessly about flowers. Her grandmother, Violet, loved flowers and had them everywhere. So, it was only natural that Zinnia would open a floral shop with the money.

As she pulled in front of her store, Zinnia smiled at seeing the neon purple sign hanging above her shop that read *Violet's Flowers*. She threw the empty coffee cup in the trash receptacle on the sidewalk and unlocked the door. A vast array of flowers greeted her as she walked in. Zinnia never tired of that morning greeting. Nor did she ever tire of the splendid fragrances that always filled the shop. She sat behind the counter, flipping through the potential employee applications, she'd planned to interview that morning.

The shop had several handmade wreathes hanging throughout and many shelves filled with flower arrangements and plants. Windchimes hung from the ceiling in one corner, while another corner of the showroom was dedicated to colorful balloons that could be added to any floral arrangement or bouquet. In the center of the shop sat a huge round table of potted violets in every shade possible, in honor of Zinnia's grandmother. The violets were the showstopper of her floral shop. They arrogantly displayed their many shades of blues, yellows, whites and creams, along with their heart-shaped leaves. There were small tables that held buckets of seasonal flowers, and along the wall near the counter was a glass walk-in cooler, which held a plethora of roses and daisies. Daisies were Zinnia's favorite.

Before the first applicant arrived, Zinnia grabbed her work apron and put it on. She had hoped it would hide her stained blouse. The first applicant was a sixteen-year-old girl with a bicycle that had a white wicker basket attached to the front of it and no driver's license. Shaking her head, Zinnia dropped the application into her special filing system hidden behind the counter next to her stool. The second applicant was a middle-aged man who reeked of alcohol, had a DUI, and likewise, had no license. Sighing, she watched as his application fluttered into the trash. The last man came with a driver's license, as well as a walker. He was eighty-three years old. She crumpled his application and tossed it in the round bin on the floor.

The morning passed rather quickly, considering the interviews she had scheduled were all the wrong candidates. She didn't know what she would do if she didn't hire a delivery driver soon. With the way her shop was picking up business daily, she didn't have the time to make deliveries in addition to running the shop. Zinnia laid her head on the counter and waved a white paper towel in the air.

"I give up!" she said out loud.

"Don't do that."

Zinnia jumped at the man's voice, knocking papers and pens from the counter in her rush. Then she recognized him.

"You!"

"Yep." He stood in the doorway and flashed a huge smile, revealing a straight row of sparkling white teeth.

"What are you doing here?" she asked, as she tried to not look like she was stepping on the pens that now littered the floor behind her desk. "Are you following me?" She noticed that his blue eyes danced with delight as he watched her try to find her feet. *Those eyes*, she thought. Why hadn't she noticed those this morning?

"I'm not following you," he said, walking further into her floral shop and letting the door close behind him. "I'm applying for the delivery driver position."

Zinnia watched him eyeing her.

"So, let me get this straight," she spoke, not quite believing he was applying for the position. "You rammed into my car this morning, made me spill my coffee, and then you just happen to show up at my shop … wanting a driving job, no less."

"Yep," he proudly answered, and winked.

Zinnia shook her head in disbelief. Her day was taking a sudden spiral downward. She needed some time to think. She bent down to pick up the pens and papers she had knocked onto the floor. "Why should I hire you?" she asked, as she squatted down. She was glad she had chosen to wear her navy-blue slacks instead of a skirt today.

"Well for starters, you don't seem to have much of a choice."

"Excuse me?" She rose at that and put her hands on her hips. She wished she hadn't decided to wear her new ivory heels. Her feet were beginning to hurt.

He shrugged. "I've been watching your candidates walk in and out." His smile was smug. "Looks like it's pretty slim pickings."

Zinnia's heart fluttered a little. "You were watching my shop, watching me and yet you say you're not following me?" She could feel the heat rising at the back of her neck.

"Okay, okay," the man grabbed the paper towel she'd used and waved it. "Truce." He set the towel back down, extending his hand in her direction. "I'm Axon."

Zinnia looked at his out-stretched hand and hesitantly extended hers, watching it disappear in his as he wrapped his fingers around hers. "I'm Zinnia," she offered.

"Now that the formalities are finished, do I have the job?"

"Here. Fill this application out first." She slid it across the counter with a pen and watched him answer the questions. Nervously, she began clicking her pen open and close continuously until he stopped writing and looked up at her, eyebrows raised.

"Sorry." Zinnia cleared her throat, setting the pen down.

"There," he said, sliding the application towards her. "Well?"

"Hmm." She contemplated as she read.

She looked at Axon. Was she doing the right thing by considering him? She really didn't have much choice. Even though she would never admit it to him, he was right. The pickings *were* slim, and she needed someone.

She sighed. "Okay, but on a trial-basis only. Be here at ten tomorrow morning."

"Cool beans," Axon said, waving goodbye over his shoulder and left.

"*Cool beans ... did he really just say that?*" Zinnia opened the drawer below the counter and slipped Axon's application inside.

CHAPTER TWO

T HE FOLLOWING MORNING ZINNIA FINISHED wiping off the small rectangle table that stood in front of the large shop window. She had plans for the space. Even though daisies were her favorite, she had a soft spot for orchids. She would send Axon to the distributor for a shipment of them later today. She had decided this would be the perfect spot to display them, in the morning sun.

As she turned around, with the wet rag in her hand, she nearly bumped into Axon.

He grinned. "Morning, boss lady."

"Axon!" she let out a huge sigh. "Do you really have to do that?"

"What?"

"Sneak up behind me ... AGAIN."

Axon shrugged. "Easy, boss lady. I come bearing a gift." He held a cup of coffee toward her. "I felt bad about yesterday." He took the wet rag from her hand and handed her the red Styrofoam cup in its place. "And look, it has a lid on it. You know ... just in case," he winked.

"Real funny," she chirped. "Thank you."

She was grateful. It was a nice gesture. Maybe he wasn't as bad as he seemed. As Zinnia took a sip of the hot coffee she glanced at Axon. He was standing close enough that she could smell his cologne. She closed her eyes and inhaled the scent before she realized what she was doing. When her eyes darted open, his eyebrows were quirked at her, with that same smug smile on his face.

Her cheeks grew red, and she nodded abruptly toward the counter. "There's a sink over there. Go ahead and toss the rag in."

"Sure thing." He winked at her, and she caught the strut in his stride as he disposed of the rag.

She set the cup down and picked up a large envelope instead. "Come with me, I want to show you the van you'll be driving." Turning on her heels, she strolled outside. Tension rolled off her shoulders as she exited the building and felt the warmth of the sun. She loved the morning sun.

As much as she loved being in the sun, she had to be careful. Her pale skin always seemed to protest. When she and Sophie were seventeen, they went to the local pool determined to get tans. It was a hot August day and they were equipped with their beach towels, sandals, and baby oil. After continuously dousing their bikini clad bodies with the oil until they shined, they claimed their spots on loungers in hopes of getting a nice tan.

At the end of the day, Sophie's body glowed as if she had just come back from a week in the Caribbean. Zinnia's didn't. In fact, her skin had little blisters forming and she turned a shade of lobster red. She ended up badly burnt and became ill with sun poisoning which landed her a few days in the hospital.

Tearing open the large brown envelope, she pulled out two large square magnets and a handful of small round decals. She placed one of the magnets on the front passenger door of the van and took a few steps back, admiring it. It was a large light purple sign with the words of her shop printed in dark purple, along with the phone number. Satisfied, she hurriedly grabbed the other one and placed it on the driver's side. Across the back of the van she placed small round decals of daisies, roses, and violets haphazardly. Stepping back to admire her work, she bumped into Axon.

"I need to buy you a cat bell," she muttered.

"Um … what are you doing?" he pointed to the van.

"Advertising." She made a face. "Anyone can see that."

"Yeah, but you expect me to drive the van with that frou-frou stuff all over it?"

Zinnia rolled her eyes. "You wanted the job."

"Boss lady …" he walked around the van, stopping next to her. "I don't do frou-frou," he said. "Just saying."

"Really?" she eyed him from head to toe, seeing the chagrin look on his face, and it made her smile. "That's apparent." Axon was much taller than herself. A Seven-

Up T-shirt, blue jeans, and flip flops completed his ensemble for the day.

She reached into her pocket, brought the keys out, and jangled them in front of him. She was enjoying the baffled Axon. "While you're driving around town making deliveries, we need to let the public know it's Violet's Flowers. If you want this job you will do 'frou-frou' ... just saying!"

Axon grabbed the keys in frustration. The fact of the matter was, he needed this job. He was in his early forties and was not a nine-to-five, dress-in-suits kind of guy. Working in the local pizzeria during the evenings, wasn't quite covering all his expenses. Other people often described him as a lackadaisical man who never grew up. He hated having to deal with the stigma just because he didn't want to be confined behind a desk.

Zinnia was, obviously, the exact opposite of him. After all, she had her own floral shop. With that, he could tell, came a vision of where she was headed in life. He guessed she was in her mid-thirties and a bit too high strung for his liking. She was his boss though, and nothing more. Even if he did sense a small spark between them. She was completely different from any woman he had known. He drank in her appearance and found her attractive. She wore very little make-up, and it suited her. She had short red hair with a lot of choppy layers and brown eyes that caught his attention. Her nose and cheeks were covered with freckles, and her lips were painted with bright red lipstick that matched her hair.

"Fine." Axon shook free of his thoughts. "Where am I headed?"

"First, I need you to take the plants sitting behind the counter to Green Funeral Home, and then I need you to take the vase of pink Gerber daises to Jefferson Hospital. The room number is written on the card I attached."

"Then?"

"Then I need you to go to the central business district to my distributor and pick up my order of orchids." She flashed him a quick smile.

His eyes lingered on her reflection in the rearview mirror. As he drove away, he realized just how dainty and thin she was.

With flowers scattered about on her worktable, Zinnia started to put together a bridal bouquet that needed finished for the morning. The order was for bright pink Gerber daises, regular white daisies, and Shasta daisies with cascading greens. She tried to concentrate on the arrangement, but her thoughts kept weaving their way back to Axon. From what she could tell he was a little older than herself. He also had a nonchalant air to himself. It flustered Zinnia while intriguing her at the same time. Such ... calm was something she wasn't used to.

"Stop it, Zinnia," she ordered herself, and ran her fingers through her short hair, messing it a bit. She was in Lower Braxton to forget, among other things, relationships. But as she picked up the green floral wire, her mind drifted back to the sapphire color of Axon's eyes and his enticing cologne. Finishing the bouquet, she placed it in the cooler alongside the other wedding arrangements she finished earlier.

"Excuse me," a lady standing at the counter said. While cracking her gum she was watching Zinnia.

Zinnia's face flushed as she walked to the counter. How long had she been waiting?

"May I help you?"

"My name is Tulu." The lady spoke through her gum chewing. "I need a simple bouquet that I can place in a cemetery urn."

"Did you have anything particular in mind?" Zinnia asked. The woman had platinum curly hair and bright pink lipstick. Both of her wrists were covered in beaded bangles that extended all the way to her elbows, and large round hoops hung from her ears.

"Nothing too fancy. It's for an old school chum of mine."

"No problem." Zinnia disappeared and reappeared with a small bundle of pink carnations. "How do you feel about carnations? Pink symbolizes remembrance."

The lady nodded. "Well, carnations were good enough for Marty to sing about, so they're good enough for me!"

"Anything else?" Zinnia asked.

"That's it, honey." The woman pulled her wallet from the denim sundress she was wearing. "How much?"

"Eight dollars." Zinnia found her refreshingly different than her other customers.

"Here you go dearie." One by one, the woman counted crumpled dollar bills, laying them next to the cash register.

Zinnia looked at the older woman's manicured nails painted with pink glitter, and tucked her own plain, natural nails into her fists.

Cracking the gum between her teeth and taking hold of the carnations wrapped in clear cellophane, the woman left the store singing about a white sport coat and a pink carnation.

Susan Mellon

CHAPTER THREE

"HERE LET ME HELP YOU with these," Zinnia offered as Axon picked up the awkward tray of wedding flowers. She opened the van door for Axon as he maneuvered the tray into the van. As he stowed the tray in the van, his arm brushed against hers. Sensation rippled through her, and she backed up.

Axon looked at her as he closed the door. "You okay?"

"Fine. Why?" She could feel her cheeks growing red.

"No reason."

"After you deliver the flowers, that's it for today. I close early on Saturdays."

"Sure, boss lady."

"Axon, why do you keep …" Zinnia stopped mid-sentence when she saw that he was wearing flip flops again.

"Why do I keep doing what?"

"Never mind that. Um. You're delivering flowers to a wedding and you have flip flops on again. Really?"

Axon looked down at his feet and laughed. "No biggie. I have a pair of loafers in my car, somewhere."

He walked to his Cobalt that was parked in front of the van. "Just a sec!"

Zinnia followed him to his car. She couldn't believe what she saw. The front passenger side had a stack of newspapers on the seat, and the floor was covered in empty fast food bags. Kneeling on the edge of the backseat, Axon sifted through a pile of crumpled T-shirts and empty pizza boxes. The floor had half empty-water and pop bottles scattered about, along with magazines. Zinnia blinked hard several times, making sure she was seeing correctly.

"Found them," Axon yelled, holding up the shoes. He slipped his feet into the brown loafers promptly and left to make the delivery.

Turning the neon sign off that hung in the window of her shop, Zinnia cringed at what she had seen a few minutes ago. Axon was a slob. How could a grown man or any adult, for that matter drive around surrounded by trash and dirty clothes? "No biggie," she mocked, exaggerating her speech to sound like him. She wrinkled her nose and dismissed the thoughts of Axon collecting in her head. The thoughts were nothing more than a tangled vine.

She usually spent Saturdays dusting, watering, and misting the plants and flowers in her shop. Flipping through the playlist on her phone, she found her favorite artist. She scrolled through the list of Annie Lennox's songs. Cranking up the volume on the phone, she left it sit on her desk. Zinnia started watering flowers and singing along to "*Here Comes the Rain Again.*"

She made her way around the shop with her watering can in hand, twirling in circles and swinging her hips to the music. At one point, she got so caught up in the music that she flung her arms wide for a final spin. Her movement caused the water from the can to slosh out, soaking the front of Axon's T-shirt. Her heart leapt into her throat and her free hand to her chest, as she saw him standing close to her in the shop.

"Whoa … that's cold!" he hollered, dodging out of the line of fire and laughing. "And yes, 'it's raining on me.'"

"Axon!" Zinnia gasped, clutching her chest. "What are you doing here?"

"After I delivered the flowers I came back for my car. You were still here, so I decided to come say bye."

She tried composing herself by smoothing her blouse and setting the watering can on the floor.

"I thought you're supposed to talk to plants, not sing to them." He folded his arms across his wet shirt.

"Well, I happen to sing to them!" Zinnia smugly answered, picking up the watering can and sashaying across the store.

"How about grabbing a burger with me?" She heard Axon call out behind her.

That stopped her in her tracks. "You mean now?" she sounded surprised.

He walked toward her, squeezing water from the bottom of his shirt. "That was the idea. You know, with it being lunch time and all."

"I never go to lunch on Saturdays. This is when I go over the shop's numbers for the week." Zinnia prided herself on a strict schedule. Saturdays was for watering the flowers and going over the ledgers. She had a list for each day of the week of things that needed done.

"You can do that after lunch." He looked at his watch. "Come on. We shouldn't be more than an hour. That leaves you plenty of time. You need to eat anyway, right?"

Zinnia watched Axon. He was waiting for her answer. He did have a point about her needing to eat, but she wasn't altogether sure lunch with him was a good idea. Theirs was a working relationship, and they probably shouldn't fraternize outside of work. Nothing good would come from it.

"One hour," she found herself answering before she could stop herself.

"Great, let's go." He took her hand and led her out the door before she had time to change her mind.

The small diner at the end of the block was extremely busy. With standing room only, they found a spot near the window that had counter space to eat at. Oldies music echoed from the speaker system, while the customers filled the diner with chatter and laughter. Zinnia and Axon ordered bacon cheeseburgers and shared an order of fries.

Zinnia dipped a fry in her cup of Heinz ketchup. "So, Axon, why do you wear flip flops all the time?" She put the fry in her mouth, leaving a small dollop of ketchup in the corner of her mouth.

Axon motioned toward the corner of her mouth. "You have a little something ..."

"What? Oh." Zinnia swiftly dabbed it off.

"In answer to your question, I like them and hey, it was good enough for Jesus to wear sandals all the time."

Zinnia's eyes squinted. That was it. That was his answer. "Yes, but he lived in the Middle East, not Pennsylvania. The weather was a lot more conducive for wearing shoes like that year-round."

"It's all good."

Zinnia wiped her hands on the napkin and tossed it in the empty basket where her hamburger was. "Okay then, what's with the boss lady comments all of the time?"

"Well, you're my boss," he said, snatching a fry.

Zinnia sighed. Talking with him was like talking to an overgrown teenager. Not to mention, his long hair and his blue jeans, T-shirts, and flip flops. The inside of his car was atrocious, and he had such a laxed attitude. She reached for the last fry at the same time Axon did, and their fingers brushed against each other. Electricity tingled through her spine, and she pulled back as if she'd touched a hot stove.

Axon had no problem dropping the last fry into his mouth, while sipping his Pepsi. "What made you open a floral shop?" he asked.

Had he even felt anything at their touch? she wondered. "Oh." She tried to smile and relax. "When I was a little girl, I visited my grandmother quite a bit. I was her only grandchild. She kept flowers everywhere. I would always help her water them, which was a pretty big job. At least it seemed like it at the time." Zinnia swallowed the last of her water. "As we went from room to room, she would talk about the different kinds of flowers or plants. I guess I fell in love with them from watching her love them so much. She left me some money, and I thought why not uproot and open a floral shop in her honor."

Axon nodded, seeming thoughtful. "Her name was Violet? That's who you named the store after?"

She nodded. "Yep. What about you, Axon?"

"What about me?"

"What did you want to do when you were growing up?"

"Never gave it much thought, to be honest."

Zinnia tilted her head and chimed, "I thought all little boys wanted to grow up and drive a bus or a firetruck or something."

Axon looked at her. "Those thoughts never crossed my mind." He shifted in his seat, and his eyes drifted. "Home life didn't give me much chance for daydreaming."

Zinnia sensed a tension in his words. "What was home life like?"

He hesitated for an uncomfortable amount of time. Then he looked at her. "Let's just say I learned self-preservation at an early age. And I never wanted a desk job. That would suffocate me. I do odd jobs to get by."

Zinnia's heart fell. For the first time, she saw a tiny glimpse of the real Axon. She looked at her watch. "It's been longer than an hour, and now I'm behind schedule. I need to go." She grabbed her purse and stood to leave, but Axon touched her elbow. Again, she shied away from the charge his touch gave her.

"Wait. Let's split a sundae."

"No Axon, I need to go."

"But there'll be a cherry on top."

"What does that have to do with anything?" she was becoming a little perturbed.

"Cherries make everything better."

Cherries? "I have work to do." She strode past him before he could say anything else.

Susan Mellon

CHAPTER FOUR

GOING OUT FOR HAMBURGERS WITH Axon threw the rest of the weekend off for Zinnia. She had known it would. Why had she gone with him? From the time she was a little girl, her parents barked at her that the only way to succeed in life was to follow a strict schedule. She couldn't concentrate on the shop's ledgers. She'd lost that time. She had other things to do too.

She gladly accepted the interruption when her phone rang. It was her best friend, Sophie. Sophie had business meetings all week and would be passing through Lower Braxton on her way to Pittsburgh. The two of them hadn't seen each other in over a year, and Zinnia thought Sunday evening would be a perfect time to catch up, especially over pizza and wine.

The two of them had been friends since kindergarten. Even at that age they bonded instantly. Zinnia remembered the first time she saw Sophie. She was completely intrigued by her blond hair. And Sophie thought Zinnia's bright red hair looked exciting. During recess on the first day of school, they declared that they would be best friends for life and even more than that, they would be sisters. They became inseparable and were known as each other's shadow.

Zinnia stood outside Tony's Pizzeria waiting for her friend to arrive. A misting rain had begun to fall. She was glad she had worn a sweater. She always chilled easily when it rained.

A white Mercedes pulled up with Sophie behind the wheel. Zinnia watched her friend get out. She was much taller than Zinnia, and extremely thin. Sophie had long blond hair that was pulled to one side of her head, tied loosely into a ponytail. Her skin was the color of cream. Sophie loved to wear make-up, the opposite of Zinnia, and her nails were Frenched manicured. Today she dressed casually, in blue jeans and a green sweater with sandals.

They hugged each other and walked into the pizzeria. The smell of baking pizza crust, pepperoni and sausage greeted them. Inside, a few tables were scattered about, dressed in the proverbial red-and-white-checkered tablecloths. Vases of Aster daisies adorned the tablecloths, and a large map of Italy hung on one of the walls. A huge brick oven sat behind the counter that cooked the pizzas, emitting a nice warmth and welcome atmosphere.

"What do you think," Sophie asked, as they chose a table away from the door. "Our usual?"

"Boss lady! What are you doing here?"

Zinnia whipped her head around at the voice. Axon was rounding the counter and headed toward them, grinning. "Oh no," Zinnia whispered. Would he go away if she ignored him?

"Who *is* that?" Sophie's brown eyes sparkled at the scene playing out before her.

"What can I get you?" Axon stood next to the table waiting for their order, smiling at both. He wore a Tony's Pizzeria apron and a name tag.

Zinnia couldn't bring herself to speak. Finally, Sophie chimed in. "We'd like a medium thin-crust pizza. Light on the cheese and loaded with pineapple, with two glasses of white zinfandel."

"Got it," Axon said, leaving to put their order in. Before Sophie could start probing Zinnia for answers, he returned with two glasses. "Your pizza will be ready in a bit. If you need anything else, just give me a holler."

"Okay, Zin, who's that?" Sophie demanded, leaning closer after he was out of ear shot.

"Nobody."

"Girl, you forget who you're talking to!" She raised her glass and took a sip of wine.

"Really?" Zinnia nervously swirled the wine in her glass. She had suddenly lost her appetite. "He makes deliveries for me. I forgot that he works here in the evenings too."

"… and?"

"What?" Zinnia asked, raising her eyebrows and taking a gulp of her wine, as if that would hold off Sophie's question.

"You know what."

"He is an employee of mine. End of story."

Sophie tapped her nails on the table, eyeing her friend suspiciously. "If you say so." She took another sip of wine. "It's so good to catch up again. It's been way too long."

Zinnia was happy to revert the conversation back to her friend. "You're in meetings all week, huh? By the looks of the car parked outside, you're doing well for yourself."

Axon set the pizza in the middle of the table. Without saying a word, he served each of them their first slice. Overhearing the comment about Sophie's car, he stretched his neck to see outside the window and whistled. "Nice wheels," he said, going back to work behind the counter.

"I'd like to think that I am doing well," Sophie said. "I took your lead and went into business for myself. I do marketing consultant work for large corporations." She smiled at Zinnia, "It's taken off!"

"That's wonderful!" Zinnia raised her glass in toast fashion toward her childhood friend. Sophie laughed, raising her glass, making them clink together. "I'm glad you decided to stop by on your way to Pittsburgh. It's nice catching up again, Sophie!"

"Long overdue," Sophie added.

"I almost forgot, how's Marcus?" Zinnia asked.

"He's doing well. He recently received an award for the top corporate bank executive in Harrisburg. Hard to believe that we've been married a year already. What about you, Zinnia? Anyone new in your life?"

Zinnia shook her head emphatically. "You know how it ended with Gage."

"That was two years ago, Zin." Sophie eyed her friend carefully. "What about him?" She nodded in Axon's direction. He was lingering behind the counter.

"What?" Zinnia laughed out loud, picking off a piece of a crust and nibbling on it. "He's an overgrown teenager."

"That may be, but I sensed something between you guys."

Zinnia rolled her eyes. "I don't know anything about him. Except for the fact that his wardrobe consists of blue jeans and flip flops and that it looks like he lives out of his car."

Giggling, Sophie snatched the last slice of pizza and took a bite. "So, ask him something."

"Such as?"

"I don't know," she shrugged her shoulders. "Ask him what his favorite vegetable is."

"You're kidding, right?"

"I'm serious." She stood, swallowing the last of her wine. "I need to hit the road. I still have a few hours ahead of me."

The two friends walked out, arm in arm. Sophie got in her car and rolled the window down. "You take care, Zin. I'll call after I get back home."

"Be safe. Love 'ya."

"Love you too." Sophie backed out of the parking space slowly. Driving away, she yelled out the window. "Remember, ask him what his favorite veggie is!"

CHAPTER FIVE

ZINNIA SLIPPED INTO HER LIME-GREEN polka-dot pajamas and pink fuzzy slippers, smiling at Sophie and what she'd suggested. There was no way she was going to ask Axon what his favorite vegetable was. *That was completely absurd*, Zinnia thought. Sure, she didn't know much about him, and she planned on keeping it that way. She shuffled into her bathroom, washed her face and brushed her teeth before returning to the bedroom. She'd seen enough of Axon to know that they were complete opposites.

In this case, opposites did not attract. Axon was a slob, and she was not. Gazing around her tiny apartment she smiled and nodded. It was in complete order, nothing out of place. She had a vision for her life, for her career. Axon worked for high-school wages.

She was not ready to open her heart again, especially after the way Gage hurt her. It took some time to get over him and start over. She needed to protect her progress. Gage made a complete fool of her. Uttering his lies while telling Zinnia he loved her.

Turning the covers back on her bed, she climbed in remembering how Axon's skin felt on hers and the reaction it created within. "No, Zinnia. Stop it," she said out loud, willing herself to dismiss the unwelcomed thoughts.

The next morning Axon walked into the shop with a cup of coffee for her.

"Good morning, boss lady. It was nice seeing you last night at Tony's." He set the coffee on the counter. "For you."

"Thanks." She was a little embarrassed at the flatness in her voice. He was being nice, after all. She picked the cup up and took a sip. The aroma was wonderful. According to Zinnia, you could never have too much coffee or chocolate.

Axon didn't seem to notice the tone of her voice. "What's on board today?"

"Oh, I'm glad you asked. Today you're going to school." She eyed his Got Milk? T-shirt.

"School?" He did a double take of her face. "You've got to be kidding?" he asked.

"Nope, not at all. Let's go." She grabbed her bag and swooshed around the counter. "Time's a wasting."

Axon followed, "C'mon, boss lady. What are we really doing?"

"I told you." His chagrin brought a smile to her face. She found herself enjoying the notion just a little too much. "Seriously though, we're headed to the central business district to my distributor."

They stood at the distributor's wall that displayed a rainbow of roses for purchase.

Zinnia dived right in. "You need to learn the different types and meanings of roses if you're going to work for me. Next month is going to be busy for us at Violet's. We have Mother's Day, proms and the start of wedding season. I expect to be making lots of deliveries and tons of rose bouquets and corsages."

"Got it," he said, rolling his eyes.

"I *saw that*, Axon." She raised her voice, slightly. "Look, you may not take my shop seriously, but I do! This is my livelihood. You need to know this in case someone asks you."

"Okay, okay, boss lady ... don't flip your wig."

She started pointing at the different roses. "Nothing says love and romance like the red rose. The pink color symbolizes admiration, sweetness, and remembrance. Red and pink are the perfect colors to express yourself in a relationship." She continued, pointing towards the white and yellow roses. "Yellow, on the other hand, shows that you enjoy a person's friendship. White is the purest rose of all, expressing innocence, and is traditionally used in weddings and to represent new beginnings."

"What about these?" Axon looked at the lavender roses.

"Love at first sight. They can be used to signify the readiness of your relationship to grow. And those peach roses," she said motioning toward them, "are about appreciation and a beautiful yet, simple way to say thank you."

"Got it."

"Great." Zinnia eyed him with caution, not sure if he was really listening to what she tried to convey. "Let's get back to Violet's. I want to show you how to prepare the roses before putting them in the cooler. I want to start training you to help more in the shop."

"Groovy."

Once they got back to the store, Zinnia grabbed the coffee Axon had brought her earlier and began to take a sip.

Axon cringed. "You can't drink that."

"Why not?"

"It's not hot anymore, that's why. Coffee's meant to be drunk hot."

Zinnia giggled, taking another sip. "Room temperature … that's the best way to drink it."

"That's not normal!" His nose crinkled, and his eyes squinted.

She ignored that. "Here." She handed him a rose and a knife. "Remove each thorn and then pull the leaves off from the bottom half of the stem. And be careful not to damage anything."

"Okie doki." Axon took hold of one of the stems, pricking himself in the process. "Jimminy Christmas, those things hurt!" he said, as he stuck his finger between his teeth.

Zinnia found herself giggling at him again. She began tackling the bunch of roses in front of her, but she found herself glancing at Axon from time to time. The distraction cost her. She slid the knife down one stem and right onto her thumb, releasing a small stream of blood.

"Ouch!" she said, bringing her thumb to her mouth. "So stupid." She'd done this thousands of times.

Axon jumped into action. He took her hand in his, ushering her to the sink behind them. Flipping the faucet on, he immersed her thumb in the cool waterfall. "This should help, boss lady." Zinnia stood frozen from the quickness of his actions. He was dabbing her hand with a towel. Then he took a band-aid from the box next to the sink and wrapped it gently around the cut. "No stitches needed, but it'll be sore for a few days."

Zinnia was bemused by Axon. All she could do was nod in agreement. One minute he was like a hippie teen, and the next he hovered over her like a parent over an injured child. Was there more to Axon than met her eye? Could Sophie be right? Should she try and get to know him better? He was a mystery to her. A mystery that Zinnia wasn't sure she wanted to unravel.

She sent Axon out to make deliveries and spent the rest of the afternoon brooding, thinking back to her conversation with Sophie. At first, she thought Sophie was joking about the whole vegetable thing, but she knew better of her friend. She also knew that Sophie would be inquiring about what vegetable takes top billing in Axon's life.

An idea came to Zinnia, and she double-checked the address on Axon's application. She knew where he lived. She passed his apartment complex every day on the way to work.

Locking the shop for the day, she got in her car with one thing on her mind. Her stomach started to stir a tiny bit, as if ladybugs fluttered around inside.

Pulling up outside the complex, she found a spot in front of the building. She turned the engine off and locked the door behind her, gripping the keys as if they were the source of some sort of superpower she needed.

She became more nervous the closer she got to his apartment. The ladybugs vacated, and butterflies moved in. *Ridiculous, that's what this is*, Zinnia thought. Reaching up, she knocked on the door. It opened just a tiny bit, and Axon poked his head out.

His eyes widened. "Boss lady! What—are you—doing here?" He opened the door just a little further and stepped into the hallway, closing the door behind him.

"I have to ask you something." Zinnia rubbed her stomach. The butterflies were gone, and relentless dragon flies took their place.

"Okay ..."

"Well," she said looking up and down the hallway feeling foolish. "Can I come in?"

"Oh, um ... well," he muttered, glancing at his closed door and back at her. "Um ... no. Not now. What's up? Can't you ask me out here?"

"I guess." Zinnia could see he was uncomfortable with her being there. Squeezing the keys tighter in her hand, she blurted it out, "What's your favorite vegetable?"

"Excuse me?" He shot right back.

"Your vegetable ... do you have a favorite?" *This is such a bad idea.*

"Um, I don't know. Never really thought about it."

"I see." Zinnia turned on her heels and darted down the hall.

"Wait, boss lady!" Axon hollered after her, rushing to her side. "That's what you wanted to ask me?"

Zinnia looked into his eyes. He must think she was a maniac. All she could do was nod and walk away again. But he grabbed her arm. His grip was strong, but not too strong that it hurt her. Just strong and confident wrapping around her arm, connecting the two of them like pieces of a jigsaw puzzle. She liked the way it felt.

"What's *your* favorite?" he countered back releasing her arm.

"Chocolate."

He laughed. "Chocolate? That's not a vegetable!"

Zinnia had to chuckle herself. "What's chocolate made from?"

"Cocoa beans." He tapped his foot, folding his arms.

"Well," Zinnia smiled. "Beans are veggies, are they not? That makes cocoa beans a vegetable, making chocolate my favorite!" She examined his reaction, taking great satisfaction from the befuddled look across his face. No more words were needed. Then she left, feeling better.

CHAPTER SIX

Zinnia was looking forward to relaxing at home Friday evening. It was a long week. She needed time by herself. Time to relax with a favorite glass of wine, her favorite music, and a tub full of bubbles. It had been lightly raining all day and continued into the evening. A fog started to roll in as the sun went down.

Zinnia hung her purse and keys on the hook next to her door and drew a bath, adding a few drops of lavender oil. Soaking in a tub full of bubbles is where she did her best thinking. She poured a glass of white zinfandel and lowered into the hot bubbles with a huge sigh. It was her escape from the world.

Taking a sip from her glass, she leaned her head back, closing her eyes. She drew a long, satisfied sigh. This was exactly what she needed. Reaching for her loofah sponge, she spotted the cut on her thumb. The bandage was still wrapped around it. She pried it off, thinking of Axon.

He had rushed to her rescue, although she didn't really need him to. It was a simple cut that she could have taken care of herself. She liked the smell of his cologne and the touch of his hands. Sometimes when they talked, she found herself mesmerized by his eyes. And all this threw up red flags that she needed to pay attention to. She needed to find a way to break free.

They were totally different. There was too much she didn't know about him and yet enough of him she already knew and didn't like. His attire was not becoming for a man in his early forties. He didn't seem to have any real goals in life concerning a job and was a complete slob. He shared a tiny bit of him, but only when she asked about his past. Yet he knew why she opened Violet's and how she drank her coffee and that she loved chocolate. She giggled remembering how she passed off her love of chocolate as a vegetable.

Her slight infatuation with Axon was not part of the plan she had for herself. The walls were already put in place after Gage. She had no intention of letting Axon break that barrier. It was safe behind those walls. But she hated to admit, there was a tiny crack forming in those walls, with Axon's name etched into it.

After her soak, she slipped into a soft cream-colored sundress with bright green palm trees embroidered on it. Picking up her phone, she started sifting through her music catalog.

The unexpected knock at the door made her jump. She laid her phone on the table and opened the door.

Axon stood there with a pizza in his hands.

"Axon!"

"Hungry?"

"What's this all about?"

"Believe it or not, I felt bad about putting you behind schedule last Saturday, so … I decided to bring you dinner."

She took a step back. "I don't know, Axon."

"It's covered with *pineapple*, just the way you like it." Both of his eyebrows raised, and he smiled.

She closed her eyes. *How can I resist pineapple pizza?*

She stepped aside, letting him come in. "Set it on the coffee table. I'll grab some napkins and drinks. Wine okay?"

"Yepper," he said, setting the pizza on the coffee table.

Zinnia felt his eyes following her as she grabbed the napkins and poured the wine.

He sat on the floor between the couch and the coffee table.

"You're allowed to sit on the couch, Axon," she chirped, joining him on the floor. Zinnia handed him the first slice of pizza, fully aware of the scent of his cologne. Trying to ignore the scent, she took a slice. The pizza hit the spot. She was hungrier than she thought. Leaving Violet's, she headed straight home to a bath. Taking another bite, she noticed he was wearing a Tony's Pizzeria T-shirt today. She watched him take another slice. They hadn't spoken at all in the last few minutes, she realized. She broke the silence, "How about a little music? I was just about to put something on when you knocked."

"Great!" he mumbled, with a mouth full of pizza.

Zinnia chose "*I Put a Spell on You.*" The music started playing, and Zinnia took another slice of pizza. As she bit into the cheese, it began sliding off her slice. She brought her other hand up to catch the cheese, but Axon was faster. Leaning in without missing a beat, he took the extra cheese in his mouth. He chewed the long strand of cheese until his lips reached hers. And like a scene straight out the Disney movie, "*Lady and The Tramp*" his lips skimmed against hers for a second. They paused, looking into each other's eyes. He tenderly kissed her again as his hands moved to her shoulders. The kissed lingered, and his fingers slipped beneath the dress fabric, softly caressing the rounding of her shoulders.

Zinnia found herself falling, enjoying the kiss and the gentle touch of his fingers. Before she knew it, her hands glided across his face, feeling his unshaven whiskers. The kiss deepened. Suddenly the song came to the end, along with the kiss they shared. Pulling away, she held the back of her hand over her lips. She wasn't sure if she was wiping the kiss off or pressing it in deeper. She looked into Axon's sapphire eyes and found her heart yearning for him to kiss her once more.

Then she caught herself and gasped. She jumped up, flushed from his kiss, and ran her fingers through her hair. "Axon, I don't know what just happened, but I think you should leave."

Axon's eyes followed her as she walked to the door and opened it. Swallowing hard, he stood and crumpled his napkin, tossing it onto the coffee table. He would leave like she requested, but that wouldn't erase what just happened between them. Nothing would. He left and she closed the door behind him.

Zinnia rolled over in bed. The morning sun pierced through the blinds, hitting her directly in the eyes. "No …" she moaned in protest, pulling the comforter over her head as a shield.

She hadn't slept much last night. No matter how much she revisited the encounter with Axon in her mind, she came to the same conclusion. She should have never allowed that kiss to happen. She needed to talk with him.

She rolled over, putting her back toward the window and lowering the comforter a bit. The wall she'd built was slowly tumbling apart, brick by brick, and she didn't know how to stop it.

Her thoughts were a potpourri of reasons why she shouldn't get into a relationship with Axon, but her heart was telling her otherwise.

Throwing the comforter off, she stumbled into the kitchen. She opened the cabinet door above the coffee maker, revealing a large selection of floral-themed mugs. She settled on a pale-yellow cup with bright-yellow tulips and poured herself a cup of coffee that was left over from the day before. The coffee went down smoothly, helping clear her mind for the day.

Susan Mellon

Zinnia pulled up in front of Axon's apartment and got
out. It was a beautiful day. The rain finally ended, and
the sun was out. Opening the back door of her car, she
grabbed the two bags of groceries, pushing the door
closed with her hip. Setting the bags down briefly, she
knocked on his door and pulled them into her arms
again.

Axon threw open the door. It looked like he'd just
gotten out of the shower. His hair was wet and a tousled
mess. He had on his usual blue jeans and T-shirt but
stood barefoot in the doorway.

His eyes widened when he saw her. "Boss lady!"

"I'd thought I'd make dinner for us and we could
talk … if you don't mind," she said, squeezing the two
bags of groceries a little bit tighter for support.

"Okay." He shrugged his shoulders. "What time
should I come over?"

"No, no, you don't understand. I was thinking I
could make dinner here. You know … at your place."
She looked over his shoulder, trying to get a glimpse
of his place.

He pulled the door completely closed behind him.
"Not a good idea, boss lady."

"Oh," Zinnia mumbled.

"Let's do it at your place." Axon hated turning her away, but he couldn't jeopardize letting her into his apartment.

"I guess." She sighed, disappointed. This was the second time he'd stopped her from coming into his place. Why? "Dinner will be ready at seven."

"Great. I'll see you then."

He opened the door just enough to squeeze through and closed it again, leaving her standing in the hall by herself.

Zinnia ran her fingers over the collection of floral tablecloths she enjoyed collecting, settling on a white cloth embroidered with light blue forget-me-nots. Her pale-yellow dishes looked nice on top of it and she added two crystal water goblets. She finished off the center of the table with a crystal vase filled with forget-me-nots.

She had a hard time staying focused with preparing dinner. Her mind kept wondering back to Axon and the secret he was keeping from her. He had such an aloof attitude when it pertained to anything personal. What was he hiding from her? Why didn't he answer any questions that pertained to his personal life? Tonight, she would try and crack open the vault to Axon's mysteries once and for all.

As she sautéed the asparagus, she drifted back to the kiss they'd shared the night before. It was completely unexpected. Her mind constantly drifted to Axon. The asparagus rolled in the skillet the way Axon rolled through her thoughts. She tried to break free, she couldn't. His eyes held her captive. His touch sent currents rushing through her and his cologne, an aquatic woodsy scent, enticed her.

The sound of her phone ringing brought her back to reality. Turning off the stovetop, she picked her phone up and saw Axon's name appearing across the screen.

"Hello, Axon."

"Boss lady, I can't come to dinner tonight, something has come up."

Zinnia's heart dropped, and a huge silence fell between them. She tried to listen for any type of background noise that might reveal a secret of his, but there was no sound, just shattering silence.

"Boss lady ... hello ... are you still there?"

"I'm here." Zinnia shook her head, letting her eyes drop from the table that was already set and waiting for his arrival. "Sure, Axon. No big deal."

Zinnia ended the conversation between them abruptly and dumped the pan of asparagus into the trash. Suddenly she had lost her appetite. Axon was hiding something. She was going to get to the bottom of it and she knew exactly what she had to do. She hated to admit it, but she was looking forward to having dinner with him. Even if it was just to tell him that whatever was beginning to evolve with them had to end.

It quickly turned into an ice cream dinner night. Opening the freezer, she grabbed a pint of triple chocolate with marshmallows, along with a spoon, and headed to her bedroom. Climbing on the bed, she picked up the television remote to channel surf.

While flipping from one channel to the next, Zinnia let her thoughts wander to how she would deal with Axon in the morning. She would not let her guard down. Axon would not sweep into her shop and sweet-talk his way out of bailing on her tonight. She had heard all the excuses before from Gage. This time things were different. She knew the signs of when she was being lied to. With that realization came resolve. She could patch over Axon's name etched in the wall.

Susan Mellon

CHAPTER SEVEN

THE NEXT EVENING ZINNIA DROVE to the local park. She relished evening walks around the beautiful lake from time to time. It was peaceful and calming. The last of the evening sun glistened on the water. Ducks and other birds began taking refuge along the edges, settling in for the night. The sky showed off majestic colors of pinks and blues as the sun began its descent.

Zinnia decided to call Sophie. It was time for reinforcements. The phone rang several times before a voice on the other end greeted her.

"Zin! How are you?" Sophie chimed.

"Okay, Soph. What about you?"

"Can't complain. What's up?"

"I need your help with something. Do you think you're able to get away for a night?"

"Well, I suppose … but I need to check with Marcus first."

"Sure, I understand. Call me tomorrow and let me know." Zinnia tried to keep her voice light and carefree. She didn't want Sophie to worry.

"What do you need help with?"

"Um. I'd rather not say over the phone."

"*Zin!*" Sophie's voice was stern. "I've known you forever and a day … what are you up to?"

"I'll tell you in due time."

"Zin?"

"Just dress in black, you know, leggings and a T-shirt."

"Why? It's not like we're robbing a … bank … are we?"

"Not *exactly*, Soph. I'll fill you in when you get here. I've got to run."

"Zin. Wait!" Sophie hollered into the phone … but all that remained was dead air.

Zinnia had planned to keep Axon busy and out of her hair at Violet's. When he came in the next morning, she busied herself by reviewing the flower order for the week ahead.

"Boss lady, what's on the agenda for today?" he casually asked.

"Oh, Axon, I didn't see you come in. Good morning." She kept her eyes downward, not wanting to get lost in his eyes that she found so tantalizing. Zinnia stuck the pen she was using between her teeth. Maybe having something to bite down on would help her stay focused.

"Look, about last night …"

"No need to explain," she curtly retorted. "I need you to clean the backroom this morning."

"*What?*"

"You know," she continued without looking at him. "Keep what I might need for the shop and toss the rest." She proudly set the pen she was gnawing back on the counter and walked around him to her office, being careful not to get a whiff of his delightful cologne. Zinnia knew she left Axon befuddled with her attitude. He wasn't the one she was worried about. It was her heart.

Axon shrugged and headed off to the back room. And she sighed with relief.

It was a quiet morning with Axon banished to the back of the shop, and she managed to get a lot of paperwork done.

Around noon, she noticed Axon walk through the shop carrying empty buckets. He took them outside and put them in his car. She rose from her seat. She didn't mind if he took the buckets. She didn't need them. But why didn't he just put them in the dumpster right by the back door?

Trying her best to ignore him, she began inspecting and watering her collection of orchids. She inhaled deeply, taking notice of the wonderful mixture of aromas they released. Closing her eyes, she enjoyed the fragrances of raspberry, coconut, and citrus. Opening her eyes, she watched Axon heading toward the front door carrying the discarded floral wire that she was throwing away.

This time she followed him to his car.

"Axon!"

"What's up?" he asked, tossing the wire onto the passenger seat and closing the door before looking directly at her.

"Why aren't you throwing all that junk in the dumpster?" Zinnia motioned to all the discarded items lying haphazardly in his car.

He looked in his windows at the stuff and then looked at her and shrugged his shoulders. "I'd figured that since the garbage wouldn't be picked up until Friday morning, I'd just throw the stuff in Tony's."

Zinnia's eyes grew large from his reasoning and went back into the shop while talking over her shoulder. "If you're finished, that's it for today."

"Oki doki, karaoke," he mumbled.

Axon stared into the case of chocolates at the Chocolate Delite's candy store, trying to decide what he should buy. He knew Zinnia loved chocolate, but he didn't know what her favorite flavor was. The case displayed many confections such as turtles, truffles, creams, nuts etc. He felt bad about having canceled dinner with her the other night. He felt even worse when she wouldn't let him explain. What was he supposed to do? His boss had an emergency at home and needed him to come to work and cover the pizza shop.

After the kiss they shared, he knew there was something special stirring. He hadn't meant to kiss her, but the fact of the matter was, he did. They both enjoyed it, of that he was sure. He also was very much aware of the fact that she was upset with him. Why else would he have been banished to the back of the shop for cleaning duty? Hopefully the box of chocolates would be accepted as an apology.

Axon's thoughts drifted back to the evening of the kiss. Zinnia moved gracefully across the large room, and the sundress she'd worn swayed and swirled over her legs. She was barefoot, and she'd tucked the short strands of her red hair behind her ears. Her eyes had sparkled as she'd sat next to him on the floor, affirming to him, that she was pleased that he was there. Her lips were bare from the usual red, revealing their natural shade of pink, which he preferred.

"May I help you?" The sales lady behind the counter interrupted his thoughts.

"That would be great," he said, scratching the back of his head. "I want a box of chocolates, but I don't know what kind she likes."

"I see. Well then, how about a small box of assortments?"

"Yes. No. I want a box of assorted truffles, a box of creams, a box of nuts and a box of turtles."

"Four boxes?"

"Yepper."

"What did *you do*?"

"That obvious, huh?"

The lady just shook her head. "Kind of."

"I broke a dinner date." Axon puffed his cheeks up with air, then released them. "I'm hoping this makes up for it."

"Well, it's certainly a start," the lady said, as she started to fill his order.

"I almost forgot do you have a card I could put with it?"

"Sure. What do you want me to write on it?"

Axon stood there for a few seconds thinking. Suddenly he knew. He smiled nodding his head. "Corn on the cob."

"Okay then," the sales lady laughed at him.

Axon paid, taking the bag of chocolates. Then he headed to Zinnia's apartment. Glancing at his watch, he knew she would still be at work. Perfect.

CHAPTER EIGHT

Z INNIA ANSWERED THE KNOCK ON her apartment door to find Sophie standing there with her overnight bag. "Sophie, I'm so glad you're here!" She pulled Sophie into her arms.

Sophie was all business. "What's going on, Zin?"

"Let's go over to the table. Hungry?"

Sophie looked at the four boxes of chocolates that were spread across the small table. "A little hungry, are we?"

Zinnia shook her head. "They were a gift from Axon. Go ahead, read the card."

Sophie picked up the small card reading it out loud. "'Corn on the cob.'" She laid it back on the table, sat down, and deposited a truffle in her mouth. "I'm confused, Zin. What's that supposed to mean?" Sophie took another piece of chocolate.

Zinnia sat down too, taking a bite of a pecan turtle while sliding a glass of wine to her friend. "That's the answer to your question."

"What question?" She picked up her glass, sipping its contents.

"You told me to ask him what his favorite vegetable was. Well, I did, and he didn't answer me … until now." She picked up the card, waving it and letting it fall to the table.

"Oh my … goodness!" Sophie almost lost the piece of chocolate she had in her mouth and burst out laughing.

"Keep laughing, Soph. Remember Project Mrs. Jacob?"

Instantly, Sophie stopped laughing and started coughing, covering her mouth with the back of her hand. "What?"

"You know what. Tenth grade."

"Well, yeah. She gave us that pop quiz because she knew if we didn't get enough answers right, we wouldn't go on the field trip. Then you wanted to break into her house and wallpaper it with maps while she was on that field trip. So what?"

Zinnia didn't answer, and Sophie's eyes met hers. Zinnia smiled.

Sophie did not smile. "You're not serious, are you, Zin?"

"I sure am."

"But why?"

"Because. I went to Axon's apartment twice, and he wouldn't let me in. He also doesn't answer any personal questions, especially about his past."

Sophie nodded. "So."

"And he canceled dinner with me, last minute." Zinnia continued. "We kissed and …"

This time Sophie interrupted. "I know where you're going with this. Axon is not Gage. You need to let this go. Every guy you meet isn't Gage reincarnated!"

Zinnia's cheeks stung with embarrassment. "Let it go, huh? Gage really hurt me. One minute he would whisper he loved me and the next minute he ran back home to his wife and kids. I will not play the part of a fool, ever again!"

"Zin …"

"Look," Zinnia stood up. "If you don't want to help me, I'll do it myself."

"Of course, I'll help you. You're my best friend, but I don't know what you think you're going to find. Do you really think he has a secret family stashed away in his apartment?"

"I don't know but we're going to find out."

Dressed in black and armed with flashlights, the two women stood outside Axon's apartment door.

"Okay, Sophie, you stand guard while I try to pick the lock."

Zinnia knelt and pulled the pin from her hair. Inserting it into the lock, she quickly turned it to the right and then back to the left. She wiggled it around loosely for a bit before hearing a small click. Then she stood, putting the pin back into her hair.

"Ta-da," she smiled, turning the knob and letting the door slowly open. "Step into my office."

Zinnia entered first and then Sophie, closing the door after them.

"I'm not so sure about this," Sophie whispered.

"You don't have to whisper. Axon's working tonight. I asked him at work today."

"Well, let's get this over with and are these really necessary?" Sophie gestured to her flashlight.

"I guess not." Zinnia began feeling for the light switch on the wall. Not feeling it, she took a few more steps in the darken room and hit her knee on something. "Ouch!"

"You okay?"

"My knee hit something … hold on … I think … I found … the lights." Zinnia flipped the switch upward and the apartment illuminated with light. "*What in the world*," she murmured as her eyes darted to Sophie and back to the apartment. Behind her, Sophie gasped.

The place was unlike anything Zinnia had ever seen in her life. There was stuff everywhere. Piles and piles of useless items stacked against the wall and small pathways leaving just enough space to be able to walk from room to room. Tall stacks of empty pizza boxes lined part of the wall, and the discarded floral wire from her shop lay on top of the tower of boxes. Huge stacks of newspapers and magazines covered the couch, only leaving room for one person to sit. In one corner of the room sat three televisions and several lamps. Laundry baskets sat everywhere, with crumpled clothes tossed inside and afghans lying in piles. On top the afghans were Macy's bags and eight bottles of Invictus. The cologne he wore.

Zinnia followed the small path to the kitchen. The sight made her sick to her stomach. The kitchen sink was overloaded with dirty dishes and the oven door left open, displaying several pots and pans inside. The kitchen counter held a huge collection of empty food containers, and balls of aluminum foil were tossed everywhere. The table was covered with toasters stacked one on top of each other.

This was the secret he was hiding, she thought. *Axon didn't have a secret family as Gage did. He was a hoarder.*

"Um … Zin … you'd *better* come in here." Sophie hollered from the other room.

Zinnia walked back toward Sophie. Then she stopped in her tracks.

Axon stood in the doorway.

Axon closed the door with a loud bang. He looked from Zinnia to Sophie with disbelief.

"Boss lady, what's going on here? I guess I need to call the Po-Po."

"No, wait! I can explain," Zinnia pleaded.

"The what?" Sophie jumped in. "What's the Po-Po?"

"The police." Axon pulled the cell phone from his pocket, looking at Zinnia's friend. She was probably forced into the shenanigans. Both she and Zinnia were dressed in black and holding flashlights. The friend looked remorseful and terrified. Axon couldn't tell if it was because she was caught red-handed or because she was coerced into participating. He pointed to Zinnia. "You've got a lot of explaining to do before I call." Turning towards Sophie he added, "You can leave if you want … but boss lady has to stay."

Axon watched and listened as the women decided it would be best for Sophie to leave. She couldn't have her name attached to the break-in while running a consulting business.

Once Sophie was out the door, Axon turned to Zinnia. "This is such a downer, boss lady." He tossed his cell phone on top of the pizza boxes and motioned towards the couch. "Sit!" She timidly obeyed, but she couldn't hide the fact that she was disgusted by the couch even as she lowered herself onto it. She kept glancing back and forth at the piles on either side of her.

He found no remorse on her face. She looked scared, maybe even embarrassed, perhaps. He walked over, sat on the floor in front of her, and pulled his knees in to his chest with his arms. "Start talking," he ordered, "This is unreal."

"I'm sorry, Axon."

"Sorry you got busted or sorry you broke into my pad?"

"Both … I suppose …?"

"It's not a question, boss lady." He watched her face scrunch up. "Which is it?"

"That I broke in."

"So, why'd you do it?"

"You canceled dinner so abruptly the other night---"

"Whoa," he put his hand up stopping her mid-sentence. "I tried explaining but you wouldn't listen."

Her face fell. When she spoke, her voice was softer. "I'm listening now."

Axon watched her hands nervously sliding back and forth on her thighs. Those were the hands that had caressed his face when he'd kissed her. Hands that had also broke into his place and invaded his privacy. "Maybe it's too late now." He saw for the first time a bit of regret in her features. "Boss lady." He watched her gnawing on her lower lip, wishing he was. He shook loose of those thoughts. "My boss had a family emergency. I was the only one he could call to cover the pizzeria."

She lowered her eyes to her knees. "Oh."

"When my friends need help, I lend a hand. That's what friends do."

"I'm sorry."

"You broke in because of that?"

"Um, not exactly."

"Then what?" Axon watched her closely. He had begun to have real feelings for her but what would become of those feelings now? How could he continue anything knowing that she couldn't be trusted? Now she knew his secret. He'd never let another person know about his collections. What if she didn't understand? What if he didn't trust her enough to share with her the reason why?

CHAPTER NINE

Z INNIA BEGAN TO FEEL UNEASY. She did not like the way the conversation was headed. Axon wanted answers. To do that she had to share her inner most self. If she told him the truth, where would that leave her? And what about him? He had put up walls of his own, and he wasn't letting her past them.

She sat for a few seconds looking at Axon, wondering how much she should really tell him. "Because ..." she started slowly, mindful of his body language. He was sitting very still, showing no emotion. "I've shared little pieces of myself with you, and any question that I've asked you was side-stepped, not to mention ..."

"Not to mention what?"

"Well," Zinnia pretended to pick lint off the arm of the couch. "That both times I was here you refused to let me in your place."

"So?"

"So, you've been in mine and ..." Zinnia stopped mid-sentence deciding not to divulge any more personal details. Rubbing her fingers, she added, "Are you calling the police, or can I go?"

"Hmm." Axon stood. "So, you like to keep track of things, huh?" Axon stood and walked to his door and opened it. "Go."

She walked toward the open door. The tone of his voice didn't sound angry as much as disappointed. "I'm merely pointing out facts." She paused to let him reply, but nothing came.

Zinnia felt terrible on the drive home. This wasn't like her at all. Why did she have to break into Axon's apartment? The whole idea of him having a secret family was ludicrous. Sophie was right. Not every guy was Gage. If she had only thought things through first.

He was an overgrown teenager. His attitude was blasé. So how in the world could he hide a family from her? She was beginning to wonder what was worse, a secret family or him being a hoarder. To make matters worse, she'd let him kiss her, and, truth be told, she'd rather enjoyed it. But whatever was beginning to happen between the two of them was probably ruined by tonight, and she had no one to blame but herself.

Zinnia dreaded walking back into her apartment. She knew what was coming from Sophie, a big fat *I told you so.* Opening the door, she saw Sophie coming out of the bathroom wearing her robe and a towel wrapped around her head like a turban. Zinnia slumped onto the couch and looked at her.

"Well," Sophie asked, sitting next to her on the couch and patting Zinnia's knee. "How bad was it?"

"Bad."

"But I'm sure after you told him about Gage he understood, right?"

"Um … I didn't exactly tell him …"

"Zin!"

"I know, I know. I couldn't." Zinnia covered her face with both hands. "What's wrong with me?"

"Nothing's wrong with you." Sophie pulled her friend's hands from her face. "You just don't want to get hurt. And if you think that you like him even a tiny bit, you need to fix this."

"How?"

"You know, I love 'ya but that, my dear, is something you need to figure out."

The next morning at Violet's it was quiet. Excruciatingly quiet. The fact that Axon showed up for work, was a surprise in itself. He stayed busy making deliveries, and when he wasn't doing that, he busied himself in the backroom. The air was filled with tension. Neither of them was willing to break the silence first.

Finally, she came and found him. "There are no more deliveries today, so …"

"Say no more, Zinnia. Time for me to bug out."

She touched his arm. "Wait. What happened to boss lady?" She hoped for one of his off-the-wall hippie remarks.

He didn't look at her. "You've changed. I've changed." Then he walked out.

The rest of the week continued the same way. Zinnia knew she'd messed up and was thankful that Axon hadn't called the police. But now he barely spoke to her and wouldn't look her in the eyes. She never thought she would miss him talking to her or sneaking up behind her. She longed to hear him call her "boss lady" again. So what if he had a relaxed attitude about life and only dressed in blue jeans and wore flip flops. Was she that shallow? Had being in a bad relationship with Gage ruined her from any hope of future relationships? She had to fix things. She had to find out where they were headed.

Axon received the call from Tony late Saturday night after the shop was closed. His boss needed his help, pronto. A water pipe had burst in the kitchen and was spraying water everywhere. They needed to get the shop back in running condition by the next day. He'd had just gotten home and was eating his favorite deli sandwich made of jumbo with mustard, lettuce, and pickles. Quickly he tossed the half-eaten meal into the refrigerator, grabbing the carton of milk. Opening it, he put it up to his mouth and took a huge swig. Just one the benefits of being a bachelor. No need to drink from a glass.

Rushing into the pizzeria, Axon was stunned to find it void of water. Instead, a trail of corn husks led to a stool in front of the counter on the other side of the shop.

"What in the world," Axon muttered, bending to pick up the first husk. Picking it up, he noticed a message scribbled across it with black marker. It read: *follow the yellow corn husks, you know, like follow the yellow brick road.* He glanced around. Tony was nowhere in sight. Grabbing the next husk, he looked at the writing: *a surprise awaits you.* Continuing another couple of steps, he picked each of the husks up as he passed them.

"Okay," he called out laughing. "Who's here, and what's this all about?" When no one hollered back he shrugged his shoulders stooping to grab the last corn husk. Sitting on the stool, he set the collection of husks on the counter. He stretched his neck to try and see who the author of the notes was but couldn't see anyone. "I followed the path!" he shouted into the empty place.

Zinnia appeared from behind the counter carrying a pizza box. She had a white chef's hat on and wore black leggings and a Tony's Pizza shirt that was way too big for her. Even with the size of the shirt, Axon could still make out the soft curves of her frame.

His eyes narrowed. "Zinnia, what's going on?"

"I have something for you."

Axon watched as she set the pizza box in front of him smiling.

"Look," he said, "Tony called me about some pipe bursting and---"

"He was in on it. Look, I know you probably wouldn't have met me if I'd called you."

"You're right!"

"So … I spoke with Tony."

"Don't you have something to do, like go over Violet's numbers or, I don't know," he snapped his fingers, "break into someone's home?"

She winced. "I know you're upset with me. I don't blame you. But aren't you curious about the box?"

"Not really." He watched her lean forward, crossing her arms on the edge of the counter and detected the scent of lavender that she liked to wear.

"I'm sorry about breaking into your apartment. I thought … I thought you … had a secret … family." She almost didn't get her words out.

"That I what!"

"I thought you had a secret family." She whispered barely loud enough for him to hear.

"That's the most ridiculous thing I have ever heard!" He shouted before bursting into laughter. "I mean, me? A family?" He started laughing again and stopped. He rubbed his hand over the back of his neck, feeling slightly guilty for laughing. He watched as a shadow appeared on her face and her lower lip began to tremble.

He reached over and touched her arm. "I'm sorry I laughed, but why would you possibly think that?"

"Because of Gage."

"Who's Gage?"

Susan Mellon

CHAPTER TEN

"I DATED GAGE FOR TWO YEARS, only to find out he was lying to me." Zinnia played with a short piece of her hair and avoided looking in Axon's eyes. "He would tell me he loved me all the while having a family on the side." She shrugged her shoulders. "When I found out, I promised never to play the part of the fool again."

"And you thought I had a family, too, because ..."

"Because you wouldn't let me in your apartment and wouldn't answer any simple questions about yourself. So ... I jumped to conclusions to protect myself from getting hurt again. And for that I am sorry, Axon."

"Wow."

Zinnia wished he would say something more than that. She wished he would *do* something. Anything. But he just sat there looking at her. She began to feel closed in. She pushed the pizza box just a little closer to him and opened the lid, revealing the contents. She had put a mound of cooked corn in the box with one red cherry on top. "Your favorite vegetable."

"I see that, but what's with the cherry?"

"Don't you remember? Because cherries make everything better." With that said, she picked up the cherry by its stem and walked around the counter, dangling it in front of his face. "Come on, don't you want it? It will make everything better again."

Axon stood, took the cherry from her and tossed it back on the corn. "Except us. You invaded my privacy and broke into my apartment. *My apartment!*"

Then he walked out.

Zinnia sat down on the stool. Looking at the cherry, she picked it up and ate it, discarding the stem. *Now what am I going to do?* she thought. Then, with tears stinging her eyes, she grabbed the pizza box and tossed it in the trash.

Leaving the pizza shop, Zinnia started walking to her car. She'd parked it at the end of the block so as not to tip off Axon. It was a beautiful night out, and the streetlights illuminated the sidewalks. People roamed about, enjoying the evening. Suddenly she began noticing all the couples. She had never done that before. She had accepted the fact that she was alone and liked it that way. It was better than getting hurt. But now she came to the realization that she missed being part of a relationship. Being alone may have been fine after Gage, but not now.

She watched as teenagers entered the movie theater. They looked happy and held onto each other in some form or fashion. Holding hands, locking arms around each other, or resting their hands in the back pockets of their dates' jeans. They knew the connection of being together. The very thing Zinnia suddenly longed for.

As she continued walking, she noticed an elderly couple leaving the small diner that she and Axon had gone to for lunch. The older couple looked content with each other. Like the teenagers, they too were holding onto each other. Zinnia guessed it was more of a way for them to keep steady on their feet, but she watched as the couple looked at one another. She could easily tell that they were still in love after spending a lifetime together.

Zinnia got into her car and laid her head on the steering wheel for a few seconds. Tonight hadn't worked. She still needed to fix things with Axon. Somehow. Someway. Turning the ignition, she put her car into gear and began driving home. Turning on the radio, the song "*One Is the Loneliest Number*" by Three Dog Night started playing. "Not funny!" Zinnia hollered in the direction of the radio. She quickly switched it off.

At home she changed into her pajamas and climbed into bed. Grabbing the remote, she clicked on the television. This was one time she needed a diversion from her thoughts. "*You've Got Mail*" was on. She continued to the next station that was playing "*Pure Country*". Skipping ahead a few channels, she stopped. Her favorite movie, "*Notting Hill*", caught her eye. Immediately she clicked the TV off. Unbelievable. Where was a good thriller or action movie when she needed one?

Everywhere she turned tonight it appeared love was slapping her in the face and pointing out that she was very much alone. There were even two stray cats cuddled together in the grass outside her apartment. Why now? Especially with Axon?

She was nothing, if not organized. She reached over to her nightstand, grabbing the pencil and pad she kept there.

She drew a line down the middle of the paper and wrote two titles on either side. Pros and Cons.

"Okay," she grumbled. "Let's do this rationally."

She started with the cons:

1. wardrobe choice
2. his hair is too long and a mess
3. talks like a teenager/hippie
4. secretive about himself
5. lazy attitude, taking everything
     with too big a stride
6. is a hoarder
7. is a hoarder

Zinnia wrote the last one twice on purpose.

Next, she focused on pros:

1. friendly

2. nice smile

3. entrancing eyes

4. smells good

5. hard worker

6. good kisser

7. attentive when cut finger

8. sent me chocolates

9. didn't call the police

10. brings me coffee

11. drops everything to help a friend in need

12. `````````

She started writing the twelfth reason but drifted off to sleep with the pencil making little scribble marks across the space.

The next morning Zinnia shuffled into the kitchen with her list. Depositing it on the table, she walked over to the cupboard above her coffee maker and pulled down a mug painted with daisies. Pouring the last of yesterday's coffee into her cup, she shuffled back to the table.

Sitting, she let her fingers dance over the selection of chocolates that were still on the table. She settled on a raspberry cream, popping it into her mouth, and took a sip of coffee. Picking up the list again, she read through the ponderings from the night before. Making lists was something she'd utilized in her life and could always count on.

She'd made lists since middle school. Which clubs to join, which boys to date, and which after school job to take. The lists made sense, at least to her. Writing things down in black-and-white couldn't be denied. Sighing, she laid the list back on the table and swallowed another gulp of coffee.

She was surprised to see the list of pros was longer than the list of cons. Although her mind was surprised, Zinnia knew her heart wasn't. But her mind had caught on to this too late, it seemed.

CHAPTER ELEVEN

THE NEXT MORNING AT VIOLET'S, Zinnia was working on an order she'd received for a floral arrangement. It was going to a new mother of twins. She had gathered pink and white roses along with pink carnations, a few bunches of baby's-breath and a mixture of greens. She put the flowers in a white vase. Her mind wandered as she worked.

She couldn't fathom the idea of having twins. That would completely throw off her plans. She envisioned having two children, a boy and girl. She even had their names picked out. The boy would be called Elliot Robert and the girl, Holly Marie. They would be exactly three years apart, with Elliot being the oldest. She and her husband would be happily married living in a large house in the suburbs with a huge wraparound porch on the front of it. He would own a law firm, and she would still own Violet's, bringing Elliot and Holly to work with her. Perhaps they would even have a standard white poodle. She'd always admired them from afar.

Stepping back to admire the vase of flowers, she added a huge pink bow to finish it off. Where was Axon? It wasn't like him to be late.

Pulling her phone from the back pocket of her slacks, she clicked his name. She was about to hit send when he walked through the door.

"Axon, I was just about to call you. It's not like you to be late." Zinnia set her phone on the counter.

"Sorry, Zinnia." He handed her a folded piece of paper. "Here."

"What's this?" She raised her eyebrows. She unfolded the paper and scanned the written words across the paper. "Are you serious?" She looked at him. His blond wavy hair still looked like it needed a comb, and today he wore a Myrtle Beach T-shirt. It had a small green-and-brown sea turtle underneath the words. He was standing still, watching her.

He nodded. "I am. I can't work with you, Zinnia, knowing what you did."

"Axon …"

"I'm giving you two weeks to replace me and then I will be beat the feet."

"Axon, is this really necessary?"

"Are those flowers for a delivery or pick up?" He kept the conversation characteristically calm and aloof from himself, as always.

Closing her eyes just for a second, Zinnia inhaled a trace of his woodsy cologne. "The delivery is going to the hospital maternity ward. The name and room number are on the card." She laid his resignation on the counter, taking the extra flowers she didn't include in the arrangement and put them back into the cooler. When she came out, she was alone in the floral shop.

Axon had never been in the maternity ward before. The hallway floor was pristine white and the walls in the corridor were painted a light beige with pink and blue murals of storks. The words to the song "*Happy Birthday*" trailed along the hall passage.

Knocking on the door of where he needed to make his delivery, he looked further down the ward and saw the huge glass window of the nursery. When no one replied to his knock, he slowly pushed the door open. The room was empty. Quickly he entered, setting the vase of flowers on the bedside stand, and left.

Walking toward the viewing window of the nursery he paused, wondering if it was a good idea or not. His thoughts prevailed, and he timidly stepped a little closer, looking at the row of babies in their little bassinets. They were tiny, and each baby was swaddled in striped blankets and wore a little blue or pink knitted cap. There were five babies aligned, three boys and two girls. They were sound asleep except for one that had begun to cry.

"Which one belongs to you?"

"What?" Axon looked at the man standing next to him. He guessed the newcomer was a little older than himself.

"The babies." The stranger pointed. "Which one is yours?"

"Oh … no way, dude … I was just delivering flowers."

"Well, this is my first." The stranger pointed to the first one in the row with a little blue knitted cap. "Look at him. I wouldn't trade Lucas for the world."

"Congratulations, that's just fab for you."

"But not for you, right?"

"I've never thought of if before …"

"Until," the man finished for him.

"Until …" Axon started and abruptly announced. "Until boss lady." He heard himself murmur her name as if she was part of his life.

"Who?"

"Ah … scratch that. It's no one important."

Axon briskly walked out of the maternity ward and right out of the hospital. He couldn't breathe. He could feel his heart racing. The faster he walked he realized he couldn't get away from what had just occurred. He tried, but her name was still with him. The name he so easily rattled off the tip of his tongue. The hot sun beating down didn't help either. He started to become dizzy and sweat began to bead across his forehead. Reaching the van, he fumbled with his keys throwing the door open. He got in, starting the engine and turning the air conditioning on its highest setting. Shifting into gear, he sped out of the parking lot, all the while seeing the images of the newborn babies.

He stopped at the local park. A little league baseball game was in session. He got out of the van and walked over to the fence surrounding the field. Lacing his fingers through the chain links and leaning his head against them was just what he needed to clear his mind. The parents of the ball players sat on the bleachers rooting for their children. He heard the swoosh of the bat and the umpire yelled, "*Strike one!*" A breeze started to blow, and Axon started to feel more like himself.

"*Strike two!*" The poor kid was trying his best to hit the ball but couldn't. "*Strike three, you're out!*"

Axon faintly heard the ump holler. Why did he feel like the ump's words pertained to him? Sure, he wasn't the marrying type. He didn't go steady with girls. And Zinnia had broken into his apartment. What had just happened to him? He'd never had a panic attack before, but he'd heard about them.

The thought of children had never entered his mind. He'd never wanted children. He only wanted to take care of numero uno. He didn't want to be responsible for another living person. He knew how that played out from his own parents. His dad always worked. Never around to do the things that fathers were supposed to do with their sons. His mother was worse. She was home, but she never wanted children. Axon learned from an early age how to take care of himself. If he was hungry, he cooked his own meals or went hungry. If his clothes needed washed, he washed them or walked around with dirty clothes. He never threw anything away. Afraid that he might need it one day, giving him a false sense of security.

Axon ran his fingers through his hair and headed back to the van. Why would those babies make him think of Zinnia?

He knew the answer to his musings. He was in love with her.

Walking into Violet's, Axon hoped he didn't look as bad as he felt. He immediately zoned in on Zinnia. She was standing behind the counter talking with a man who looked a little older than he. Whatever they were saying, he could hear her giggling and watched as she touched the man's upper arm.

He didn't like watching the interaction between them. It made his stomach twist in knots. He watched her take a small snippet of her hair, playing with it as she sometimes did, and her amber eyes danced in the light as she laughed. She wore a bright yellow sundress that clung to all the right curves. The bangles she wore on her wrist moved with ease as she did, softly jingling. Axon found himself longing to kiss her bright red lips.

The man she was talking with was about the same height as himself. Axon noted, doing a quick scan of him, he had brown short hair that was beginning to gray around the temples and brown eyes. He was dressed in a red polo shirt and khakis with tan loafers. Axon also took notice of the fact that he was not wearing a wedding ring. Why did that bother him? He never cared about that before, but this time it was different. He was in love.

Feeling like he was intruding at his own place of employment, he loudly cleared his throat, announcing his presence while walking towards the counter.

"Axon ... you're back!" Zinnia sounded surprised to see him. Without missing a beat, she reached up, touching the man's arm again. "I want you to meet Trevor. He's Violet's new delivery driver."

"Well, that's just ... just ... gnarly," he retorted, tossing the keys onto the counter and turning on his heels.

Zinnia excused herself from Trevor and chased Axon out the door and onto the sidewalk. His stride was too fast for her to keep up. "Axon, wait!"

He began walking faster, putting more distance between them. She watched from behind as his wavy hair moved in the breeze, trying desperately to catch up with him. "Stop, Axon!"

He stopped, turning to face her.

"Axon, what was that all about?"

"Nothing."

"Don't tell me nothing. Talk to me, *please*."

"Okay." He glared at her. "It sure didn't take you very long to replace me, did it?"

"What?" She took a deep breath. "What was I supposed to do? You're the one who put your resignation in. I didn't."

"A two-week resignation, not two hours, Zinnia!"

The people walking on the sidewalk slowed as they passed, trying to catch a small snippet of their confrontation.

"Axon, you're being ridiculous."

"Am I? Well, you won't have to worry about me being ridiculous anymore. And for the record, I was going to retract it!"

"Retract what?" she challenged.

"My notice!"

"Axon …" she blew a puff of air, making her bangs flutter in the aftermath. "I didn't … know. Why would you do that? I thought you were upset with me."

"I am … but …" he didn't finish.

"But what?" Zinnia asked. She watched him, waiting for any type of clue that might give away what he wanted to say, but there were none. She stared into his eyes as he crossed his arms over his chest.

"Because … I …" he stopped.

"You what?" She probed him to divulge what he was so desperately holding onto. She watched as he opened his mouth to continue but said nothing.

His eyes squinted as he looked at her and whispered loud enough for her to hear. "It doesn't matter now." And he turned, leaving her standing on the sidewalk.

"I'm being ridiculous." Axon mimicked Zinnia's comment to him. Armed with a box of large garbage bags, he pulled the first one out and began to fill it with the empty butter and whipped topping containers he'd saved over the years. "I'm tired of people around here thinking I'm the town's joke. I can just imagine what Zinnia thought of my pad when she broke in," he sputtered.

Next, he tossed the balls of foil and all the toasters, except for one. The others needed to go. Tying the bags shut, he looked at the mound of dirty dishes in his sink. Turning the hot water on, he took a dish cloth and tackled the dishes. He washed and dried them, then put them in the cupboards where they belonged.

As he opened the refrigerator, his nose scrunched up at the pungent odor. Tossing everything into another bag, he got down on his knees with the wet rag and scrubbed the inside until the mystery of the horrid smell was gone. Taking hold of the large bags he headed outside to the dumpster. Tossing the clutter was only the beginning of his healing. He was surprised at how refreshing it felt to ditch the stuff.

Things were different in his life now. Axon wanted more. He wanted Zinnia.

That evening Zinnia couldn't go home to an empty apartment. Usually she welcomed it, but after the exchange of words with Axon on the sidewalk, she needed to clear her head. The local park was the perfect spot to do that, and then she would head home to soak in a tub full of bubbles. It was time to double down on her relaxation techniques if she hoped to get any sleep that night.

It had been hours since she'd talked with Axon, and her head was still spinning. She watched the children playing while she did her laps around the lake. The children were picking dandelions and blowing on them. They watched with delight, as the dandelions fluttered and swirled in the air. Zinnia observed the children closing their eyes and uttering their wishes toward the little floating seeds, hoping their whispered dreams would come true.

If it were only that simple, she thought. *If only her grandmother was still here.* She missed talking with her. She was completely confused with Axon. He had announced he was leaving Violet's, and she needed to replace him. Luck just so happened to be in her favor. After Axon left to make the delivery at the hospital, Trevor came in. It was his wedding anniversary, and he wanted a special bouquet for his wife, Lisa. He mentioned to Zinnia, that he was laid off and was looking for another job to help make ends meet.

Zinnia took a leap of faith and hired him on the spot, thinking she was doing Axon a favor. With Trevor on board now, Axon could leave sooner. After all, that is what he wanted. He had been walking around these last several days upset with her. She couldn't blame him. She would be highly upset if the shoe was on the other foot. Zinnia was just thankful he didn't call the police.

Walking a bit faster she tried to keep up with her thoughts. She gave Axon what he had wanted, and he was still upset with her. She couldn't win with him. She had tried to make amends, but he wasn't interested.

Stopping at a small cluster of dandelions, she reached down and took hold of one. *It certainly couldn't hurt,* she thought. Closing her eyes, as the children did, Zinnia made a secret wish and blew all the little seeds from its stem.

She was tired now. Hopefully that meant she would sleep. She didn't have any answers. But her wish made her feel a little better.

"Just what happened to Axon when he was out making that delivery this morning?" she asked herself, as she headed in the direction of her car.

Susan Mellon

CHAPTER TWELVE

A FEW WEEKS HAD PASSED SINCE Zinnia had last seen Axon. She replayed their sidewalk conversation over in her mind, and it still made her heart sink. E*nough brooding Zinnia. Pull up your big-girl panties and move on.* Axon had moved on, apparently. She had enough to do today without pining away about Axon. Before Trevor left to make the deliveries for the day, he set up an eight-foot table on the sidewalk in front of the large picture window.

Sidewalk days had started in Lower Braxton. All the local businesses set up tables or racks outside their stores, and customers did their shopping outside. Zinnia loved this, fondly remembering her hometown. Once a year, the businesses did the same thing. She and her grandmother would spend the day going through town stopping at the many different businesses exhibiting their wares. Each of them would come home with bags filled with treasures they had discovered during the sidewalk sales. The two of them even topped off the day with lunch out on the town.

Zinnia caught herself tearing up a tiny bit thinking of her grandmother and those simpler times. She wished Violet was here to see the floral shop that was named after her. She wondered if her grandmother would be as proud as Zinnia was, right this second. Quickly, she scanned the sidewalks for the familiar face of Axon as she set the last of her flower arrangements on the table. Sadly, he was nowhere in sight.

Smiling and chatting with her customers as she made her sale's transactions helped to take her mind off him. Zinnia noticed a young mother trying to shop, but her daughter apparently had enough and was making it very clear to everyone around them that she wanted to leave. She kept tugging at her mother's arm, whining. The young mother looked exhausted.

Zinnia knelt in front of the girl who looked to be about six years old. "Hi, sweetie."

"Hi," the girl answered shyly, taking refuge behind her mother's leg, peeking back at Zinnia.

"My name is Zinnia, what's yours?"

"Trista."

"You're not having much fun shopping with your mother, are you?"

"*Noooo!*"

Zinnia chuckled, grabbing a bright blue pinwheel from under the table and extending it towards the girl. "Maybe this will help." Trista eagerly snatched it from her hand and started blowing on it, forcing the wheel to spin. She squealed with delight. "You have to promise to let your mom shop without any more whining. Can you do that?"

"Uh huh," the girl mumbled.

Zinnia stood smiling at the mother, and the woman mouthed the words, *thank you.*

Zinnia turned around, nearly bumping into Axon.

Her heart jumped into her throat. "Axon!"

"Hey," he said, extending the ice cream cone he was eating. "Bite? This ice cream is outta sight."

Zinnia looked at the chocolate ice cream cone and back at him. His blue eyes sparkled. She missed seeing him every day at Violet's. He still wore a T-shirt and blue jeans and seemed as mysterious as before. It had been weeks since she'd heard from him, and then he showed up offering her a bite of his cone? Zinnia rolled her lips inward and leaned forward without saying a word. She took a small bite of the chocolate ice cream, leaving a trace on the corner of her mouth.

Axon pointed toward the ice cream. "You have a little something," he muttered, leaning closer to her.

The closer he got, the faster her heart beat. It was beating so fast that she thought it was going to burst through her chest. A little bit closer, and she could feel her chest rising with anticipation. Zoning in on his lips as they came closer and closer, her mouth slightly opened, ready to accept his lips against hers. She stopped breathing, even felt faint with what was about to happen. Hoping and wanting him to kiss her. From the corner of her eyes she saw his hand reach up. Instead of kissing her, his pinky finger ran over the smudge of chocolate, erasing it. Then he turned suddenly and walked away.

Axon headed toward Tony's Pizza, very proud of himself for getting that reaction from Zinnia. So much so, that he felt like he was strutting on the sidewalk as a peacock would, with its plume of feathers spread wide for everyone to admire. He did know, however, that she wanted him to kiss her as badly as he wanted to kiss her.

It would have been so easy to kiss away the chocolate in the corner of her mouth, but instead he chose to wipe it clean with one swipe of his finger. He thought back to the kiss they had shared while eating pizza and knew full well the next time he felt her lips against his, he might not be able to stop as quickly as he did before. There were two things left for him to do. That was to find out how she felt about Trevor. Then to find out, if she was in love with him as he was her.

A few days had passed since that day on the sidewalk with Zinnia. Axon found himself not sleeping at night. It was time to find exactly what was going on with her and Trevor. He rolled over in bed, propping himself up on one elbow and scanning his phone for her number. Selecting her name, he put his phone on speaker, letting it lie next to him in bed.

"Hello," the familiar groggy voice answered. "Axon ... do you know what time it is?"

"Sorry, Zinnia, I couldn't sleep." He quickly glanced over to the alarm clock sitting near his bed on the nightstand. Wincing, he noticed it was two-thirty in the morning. "I'm sorry for the lateness of my call."

"Are you alright?" she muttled through a yawn.

"What, oh yeah, fine. Can you stop by my place tomorrow evening?"

"Your place, for what?" Zinnia sounded wide awake now. What could he possibly be thinking? Why couldn't this question have waited until the morning? He was being mysterious again. Her mind darted off on a rabbit trail going in every direction. Every direction, but the one she was currently supposed to be on.

Axon winced at that, too. He had been standoffish to her. He hadn't been fair.

"Zinnia?" Axon asked. No answer came. So, he tried again. "Zinnia!"

"Huh?" She was back. "I'm sorry. Um ... sure I can stop by. Can you tell me what this is about?"

"I'd rather wait. See you around nine?"

"Okay," she said. "Nine."

He didn't like how small her voice sounded.

Zinnia ended the call and drifted back to sleep.

Unlike Axon, who was more awake than before.

Susan Mellon

CHAPTER THIRTEEN

ZINNIA KNOCKED ON HIS DOOR at nine exactly. She did not want to be early, and she didn't relish the idea of being fashionably late. Axon opened the door, greeting her with a smile, a wave of his arm, and a quick bow.

"Come on in."

Zinnia looked at him. There was something very different about him tonight, although she couldn't quite put her finger on it. Walking in, she stopped in her tracks. She looked at Axon, walked back to the door, opened it, and looked at the apartment number. Seeing it was indeed his place, she shut the door, and her hands went to her face, covering her nose and mouth.

Slowly she followed Axon to the couch and stopped. She couldn't believe what she was seeing. His place was in immaculate condition. Not so much as a crumb out of place. Spinning in a circle, taking in the whole scope of things, she noticed everything was gone. All the pizza boxes, newspapers, magazines, extra lamps, televisions, laundry baskets, etc. His place was in pristine condition, including the kitchen.

She looked at Axon as he sat down on the couch, lacing his fingers behind his head with a satisfied smile. When she first entered his apartment, she'd thought she was in the wrong place. She watched as he folded his leg over his other leg. Axon wasn't wearing his usual attire. Instead he had replaced them with a green polo shirt, khakis and tan loafers.

Her hands fell from her face to her side as she blinked hard several times. She watched as he pulled his hands from behind his head and patted the seat next to him on the couch. Timidly she lowered herself next to him. She sat on the edge, facing him, so she could see his eyes. His wonderful sapphire-blue eyes. Those eyes seemed to hypnotize her each time she allowed herself to get lost in them.

"You like?" Axon spoke first and slid to the edge of the couch to be closer to her.

"Of course, I do. Your place is amazing. You've been busy these last few weeks."

"Yeah." Axon took a deep breath. "It's a tough habit to break. Growing up I had to fend for myself. So, I learned to save everything."

Zinnia began to feel nervous. Everything was different, from his dress to his apartment, to the way he seemed to intently look at her. Sitting next to him, she could smell his cologne. At least that hadn't changed. She felt like she was being swallowed up in quicksand. Clearing her throat, she somehow managed to ask him a question. "What did you want to talk to me about?"

"Trevor and you."

Her heart stopped. "What?"

"What's going on between the two of you?"

She recovered herself. "Excuse me?" she asked sternly.

"I mean to say, are you two an item?"

"What!"

"You know … are you the bacon to his eggs, the chocolate to his peanut butter, the shoelace to his tennis shoe?"

Zinnia shot up off his couch instantly. "That is the most insane thing I've ever heard in my life, Axon!"

"Whoa, calm down!" He stood. "Cool your jets!"

"Cool my jets! Calm down!"

"This isn't going so well." He put both of his hands up. "I mean to say, you hired him really fast, and I thought there might be something going on with you guys."

She rolled her eyes. "He's married. Happily married, I might add. He came into my shop to order flowers for their anniversary." She glared at him. "We already went through this a few weeks ago on the sidewalk. Remember? If not, everyone that was on the sidewalk that day probably does. I'm leaving now."

Zinnia was furious with him. He had changed his wardrobe, cleaned up his apartment, but Axon was still Axon. The same guy that infuriated her. The same guy she couldn't stop thinking about. The same guy that she wanted so desperately to kiss again. The same guy she was beginning to fall in love with and who just didn't seem to care.

Seething, she started walking to the door, but her ankle bumped the corner of the couch. It was enough to throw her balance off, and she fell to the floor. Pain shot through her ankle, and she sat up and grabbed it.

"Axon, my ankle!"

The pain was unlike anything she felt before. She had never broken a bone before.

Axon jumped into action, scooping her up in his arms and setting her back on the couch. "Oooh," she moaned. Her head swam with the sudden pain. "Is it broken?"

"I'm not sure. Maybe. We've got to put ice on it, right way. It's already starting to swell." He pointed at her. "Don't go anywhere." Turning toward the kitchen, he stopped and looked at her. "Sorry, of course you're not going anywhere, Zinnia."

"Axon ... the ice!"

She watched him disappear into his kitchen, returning with a bag of ice. He knelt on the floor by her ankle. She watched Axon make a face, while placing the ice on the bruising. It took the edge off the pain, and she could focus on her surroundings again. His fingers were sure and tender. But the concern on his face was what captured her attention. He cared about her. He *had* to!

Remembering, Zinnia lifted the finger he had bandaged all those weeks ago, examining it for any remains of a cut. There were none. "The ice feels good. Thanks, Axon." She felt embarrassed by her earlier drama. The pain was bearable. "I can probably walk on it now."

"No can do. Just sit there for a little bit. If the swelling doesn't go down, I'm taking you to the hospital to get checked."

"That's a bit extreme. It's probably just sprained or something." She pushed the ice off with her other foot, swinging both legs over the edge of the couch. "Look. Watch. I'm fine." She made it two steps before she swayed back and forth and then felt Axon's arms wrapping around her waist. She closed her eyes, partly from the pain running up her leg and partly from being that close to him. Axon's arms felt good around her waist. They were strong and firm and the only thing keeping her upright.

Without thinking, she slipped both her arms around his neck for added support. Opening her eyes, she found herself nose to nose with him. She held her breath as she watched him lean in a little bit closer and then lower her back onto his couch.

His eyes were chiding. "The ice only deadened the pain. You can't even walk on that ankle."

She blushed. "I'll be fine. Just help me get to my car."

"The way I see it, Zinnia, you have two choices."

She let out a big sigh of disgust. "And what might those be?"

"Let me take you to the emergency room, or I can take you to bed."

"*What?*" She clamored a bit loud from his last statement.

Now he blushed. "Well, not literally. I meant I will take you home and put you into bed. Your bed. Alone."

Zinnia swallowed. *Of course, that's what he meant, stupid.*

"I'm waiting for your answer."

He interrupted her daydreaming, bringing her back to his couch.

She looked at him, trying to figure out what was going on in that head, but she couldn't. Axon looked determined. "You win. Take me home."

"Marvy."

CHAPTER FOURTEEN

AXON CARRIED ZINNIA TO HER car and again into her apartment. Once inside, he carried her straight into her bedroom. Very delicately he lowered Zinnia onto her bed, smelling a twinge of the lavender she liked to wear. He wanted to nuzzle her neck and take in the delightful scent. He also knew that once he started, he would want to shower her with kisses. Instead, he reached up, tucking a piece of her hair behind her ear. Taking her hand in his, he lifted it to his lips, placing one subtle kiss on the top as a prince would do for his princess.

Reaching over her, he grabbed the extra pillow and placed it under her ankle. Then he marched into the kitchen and filled a bag with ice for her ankle.

"This will help some." He sat on the edge of her bed, gazing into her amber eyes. "Try and get some sleep. I'll be here if you need anything."

"But … you can't … sleep here," she stuttered.

"I'm spending the night. You can't be left alone."

"But …"

"On the couch," he added quickly. "I …"

"You … what?"

Axon stood. "Nothing. I'll be on the couch. Holler if you need anything."

He forced himself to put some distance between them. Stretching on the couch, trying to become comfortable, he smiled thinking of the look she had given him after he had announced his plans to spend the night. Axon was finding it more onerous to keep his feelings to himself. He always seemed to think it was an inopportune time to express the feelings he had for Zinnia.

He wanted to tell her that he was in love with her, but the time had to be right. He didn't know how much longer he could keep his feelings to himself. If only she hadn't fallen at his place. That had changed the whole course of the evening. Before the accident, he'd envisioned telling her his feelings after he'd found out there was nothing going on with Trevor. In his mind, at least, Zinnia would reciprocate the same feelings.

Now he would have to wait just a little longer before sharing with her how he truly felt.

Zinnia awoke to the sound of bacon sizzling on the stove and Axon moving around in the kitchen. He was opening and closing cupboard doors looking for what he needed to prepare breakfast. Suddenly he appeared in her bedroom doorway as if he had a sixth sense that she was awake.

"Morning," he stated, coming closer. "Hungry?"

"Mmm … it smells delicious." Her eyes followed the path of his unshaven chin. She would never admit it to him, but she rather liked the look on him.

"Good." He bent down, swiftly picking her up and carrying her to the table.

Zinnia looked at the table that he'd already set. The dishes and coffee cups were placed on top of floral placemats. In the center stood a white glass bud vase with a few daisies and baby's-breath protruding from the top. She watched as he placed the brown, crisp bacon on the plates and then added the fluffy scrambled eggs and toast. He placed juice glasses on the table and then grabbed the carafe of coffee, pouring her a cup.

"Just the way you like it," he said, returning it back to the coffee maker before sitting next to her. "Eat up."

"Axon …" She barely whispered, clearing her throat to hold back a few tears. A reaction that she was even surprised by. "Everything looks beautiful. Thank you."

They finished eating in silence. Neither knowing exactly what to say to the other. Zinnia swallowed the last of her coffee and laid her napkin on the table. "Thank you for everything, Axon, but I must get to work now."

He shook his head. "You can't go to work in your condition."

"My condition?" She winced as she tried to move her injured leg. "My ankle is only sprained. I have a business that will not run itself."

"Why can't you close your shop for the day?"

"Axon, this my job! I can't just close it because my ankle hurts. Violet's is my responsibility. Besides, I have a huge order of daisies that need to be adorned with glitter."

"Okay … okay, you're getting too jazzed. Stand up."

"Excuse me?"

"Stand up. I want to see you stand and walk on your ankle." Axon pushed his chair back and stood near her.

"This is idiotic."

"Show me that you can do it, and I'll leave you alone," he challenged.

"Fine!" Zinnia retorted. "I still say this is wacky." She pushed off the top of the table with both hands, standing slowly. Breathing out, she cautiously put her weight on her ankle. "There, are you happy now?"

"Walk."

"What?"

"Take a couple steps toward me." Axon twirled his hand in a circular motion with his index finger pointing downward.

"This is just plain silliness now." Zinnia could feel herself growing flustered with his indignation attitude. Looking at him for a few seconds, she wondered how she allowed herself to get in this situation in the first place. And how did he assume it was okay to just spend the night at her place? Even if it was innocent and it

THE FRAGRANCE OF LOVE

was the year 2019, she could only imagine what her neighbors thought about seeing his car parked outside all night.

She took a step toward Axon and swayed a bit. Her swaying caused Axon to reach forward, grasping both of her upper arms to keep her from falling.

"I'm fine, Axon, really." She fought hard to ignore how strong his hands felt on her arms and the sensation that traveled to her fingertips from his touch.

"Okay, boss ... I mean Zinnia." He released his hands and walked to the door, letting her fend for herself. He watched her immediately take hold of the chair to keep from teetering. "Have it your way." He opened the door. "Go to work, I'll leave you alone." Then he left.

Zinnia collected everything she needed to add glitter to the daisies. The local dance school had a huge recital later and had requested several bouquets with silver, gold, and purple glitter sprayed on the flowers. She pulled a stool up to the counter to work. She was able to get around slowly with her ankle but decided to sit for a little while to take the strain off of it. Tackling the bundle of daisies made the afternoon go by much faster than she realized. She rolled the finished flowers in several different colors of tissue paper, tying bows around them.

Stacking them on the counter near the register, she took notice of one single daisy lying by itself. Picking the stem up she smiled, remembering what she used to do with the daisy petals when she was a young girl. She turned her back in case a customer walked in.

Holding the stem with one hand, she slowly picked off one white petal at a time, letting each float to the floor. "He loves me … he loves me not. He loves me … he loves me not." She continued around the head of the daisy until there were only two petals left to pick off. "He loves me …" A flood of sorrow washed over her, knowing which verse came next with the last little petal. "He … loves," she heard her voice crack.

At that very moment, a man's hand reached over her shoulder, pulling off the last petal. "He … loves his boss lady, very much!"

Look for my next book
Candlelight and Pancakes

www.susanmellon.com
susan mellon facebook

ABOUT THE AUTHOR

Susan Mellon lives northeast of Pittsburgh, Pennsylvania with her husband, Alex. When not writing, Susan enjoys watching movies, vacationing in Walt Disney World, jaunts to New York City, live theater, Pirates baseball and chocolate.

Made in the USA
Middletown, DE
27 September 2019